For Alfie and Ted and their great dad, Greg
– Adam & Charlotte Guillain

For Jussie, who loves a party!
– Ada Grey

EGMONT
We bring stories to life

First published in Great Britain 2019 by Egmont UK Limited,
The Yellow Building, 1 Nicholas Road, London W11 4AN
www.egmont.co.uk

Text copyright © Adam and Charlotte Guillain 2019
Illustrations copyright © Ada Grey 2019

Adam and Charlotte Guillain and Ada Grey have asserted their moral rights.

ISBN 978 1 4052 7750 1

A CIP catalogue record for this title is available from the British Library

party for Dads

Adam & Charlotte
Guillain

Illustrated by Ada Grey

EGMONT

One morning, Anna cried, "Whoopee!
Today's your special day!"
She gave her dad a card and said,
"Come on – it's time to play!"

"I have to go to work!" said Dad.

"I'm late – I've got to run!"

"But it's your birthday," Anna sighed.

"You should be having fun!"

"Dad needs to have a birthday treat,"
She thought. "It's only right.
I'll teach him how to have some fun –
Just wait until tonight!"

She called her friends. They all came round
To help her plan and bake.

They wrote out invitations

and they iced a massive cake.

Soon after work, their dads arrived
And huddled by the door.
"Get off your phones!" cried Anna.
"You don't need them any more!"

She lifted up a box and said,
"It's time to have some fun.
We'll start by putting costumes on –
There's one for everyone."

Next Anna cried, "Let's play a game!
Watch first and then join in."

"That game looks great!" cheered Anna's dad.
"I really want to win!"

"It's your turn now," the children said,
"To make balloons go pop!"
So each dad grabbed a big balloon
And . . . sat down on the top!

BANG!

"You know the next game," Anna said.

"Just try to find a chair."

But, when the music stopped, the dads
All pushed and yelled, "Not fair!"

The dads loved Pass the Parcel, but

One called, "You're much too slow!"

Another moaned, "Just pass it on!
I haven't had a go!"

"We'll have a race now," Anna said,

"So all get into teams."

The dads became quite silly as

They raced with shouts and screams.

"Sshh! All calm down, please!" Anna cried.
"Sit still! Don't talk or giggle.
It's time for Sleeping Lions now."

The dads began to wriggle . . .

Then some dads shouted, "No! Let's dance!"
"Yippee!" cheered Anna's dad.
"But dads can't dance!" the children gasped.
"They're really, really bad!"

The dads began to shake their stuff,
To wiggle, spin and hop.
"Let's give them scores," said Anna. "Quick!
Or else they'll never stop!"

The children held their scorecards up.

The dads all gave a **ROAR!**

"I thought I'd get a ten," moaned one,
"But MY son gave me FOUR!"

At last they got the dads to sit
All quietly in a row.

Then Anna said, "It's time to watch
My special magic show!"

As Anna did each trick, the dads
All gasped and gave a cheer.

"And now," said Anna, "watch – ta-dah!
A rabbit will appear!"

"Oh, no!" she wailed. "It didn't work. Don't laugh! It isn't funny."

Her dad hopped up. "Don't fret," he said,
"I'll be your magic bunny!"

"Phew! Thanks so much, Dad!" Anna laughed.
"Now, find yourself a seat.

Your birthday tea is ready and
It's time for you to eat!"

The dads pulled party poppers and
They piled their plates up high.
"I feel *SO* sick," groaned one poor dad.
"I've eaten too much pie!"

Then everyone went quiet and
A boy switched off the light.

As Anna carried in the cake,
The candles twinkled bright!

The dads sang "Happy Birthday" till
Her dad laughed, "That's enough!"

He blew out all his candles with
One great enormous puff.

Then Anna passed the cake around
And said, "We're nearly done.

Before you go we'd like to give
A prize to everyone!"

Then Anna's dad looked sad and asked,
"Is there no prize for me?"

"Of course!" said Anna, smiling wide.
"I'll tell you what you've won . . . "

"This medal is for you because

You're best at

having fun!"